From the Book of Atmospheres

by

Robert Scotellaro

BAMBOO DART PRESS

LOS ANGELES † NEW YORK † LONDON † MELBOURNE

From the Book of Atmospheres by Robert Scotellaro
ISBN: 978-1-962316-13-2
eISBN: 978-1-962316-14-9

First Printing 2025
Cover art by Dennis Callaci
Layout and design by Mark Givens

For information:
Bamboo Dart Press
chapbooks@bamboodartpress.com

Bamboo Dart Press 054

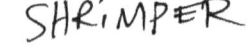

www.pelekinesis.com   www.bamboodartpress.com   www.shrimperrecords.com

for Diana

Acknowledgments

Grateful acknowledgment is made to the following publications in which these works or earlier versions previously appeared:

"Forest Nuns in the Wild" *South Florida Poetry Journal*

"Who We Are and Who We Wish to Be" *Elm Leaf Journal*

"The Verbose People of Llama" *10 BY10*

"Ledge at the Edge of the World" *South Florida Poetry Journal; Quick Adjustments*

"Headlines" *The Daily Drunk; Ways to Read the World*

"Divine Intervention" *Pure Slush Anthology*

"Metaphors Incognito" *South Florida Poetry Journal; Quick Adjustments*

"From the Book of Saints" *Defenestration; Measuring the Distance*

"Count on It" *South Florida Poetry Journal*

"High Fidelity" *Tuesday Shorts; Tuesday Shorts Anthology; Six Sentences; Nothing Is Ever One Thing*

"We all walk in mysteries. We are surrounded by an atmosphere about which we still know nothing at all."
—Johann Wolfgang von Goethe

"Our imagination flies—we are its shadow on the earth."
—Vladimir Nabokov

Contents

The Verbose People of Llama

They are a hardy bunch that dwell in a remote Peruvian mountain village. I've been allowed in. The only outsider who has. Perhaps it is the confections I bring in the shapes of exotic animals they've never seen, in combination with my long blond hair they delight in running hands through. "Lla," they say, which can mean: glorious, precarious, gregarious, flatulent... According to the way it is accented. The way the mouth wraps around each articulation, the way the face is in concert with what is spoken along with hand gestures. For there is only one word comprising their entire language. The word: *Llama*. They use every combination of its letters to great effect and are exceptional conversationalists. The poets there can wring your soul to tears with the power of their imagery and metaphors, their intimacy with the ineffable.

I have a lover there. Her name is Ama. During lovemaking she cries out, "*L-l-l—lll---l!*" I echo it back. It is a standard lustful reaction the villagers have here. Later, she recites poetry that moves me in indefinably profound ways. There are beats of silence in their language between the words/the letters. It is precise. Two seconds of silence instead of three can change the meaning, in some cases, disastrously. I said ma---la once with an inadequate amount of pauses and nearly lost my head.

Their shaman is a willowy fellow who uses his eyebrows and lip gestures when he speaks, so flexibly/so expressively, he is considered their scholar. His teachings are scripture. Ama has tutored me in properly addressing him as La-ma---la. The beats of silence, in this instance, are critical. He looks at me sometimes suspiciously, but he cured my "Frog's thigh" as it translates in their language. A nasty bit of fungus that, thank heavens, doesn't travel higher.

Occasionally I take the long journey down the mountain into town for supplies and have more specialized confections made. I've got a lover there too. Her name is Abigail. It's refreshing not to be so careful with language and facial gestures. To lie there afterwards and talk freely. And, indeed, the conversations are adequate enough. But, *Ml-a-mama—lamm!* I sure do miss the poetry.

Hotheads

Fire develops a brain with a low IQ. We try to teach it to burn only sorrow and the troubles of the world, and it does for a time, then creates troubles of its own. It boils swimming pools and some waterways and threatens the ocean with fiery bravado. But in that case, it's obvious it's overcompensating and it is just bluster born of insecurity and overreach. Small fires are not as problematic. We can keep them in metal cradles and rock them to sleep using oven mitts and singing lava lullabies. It is never completely dark anymore outside for there is always a fire somewhere showing off. The sun is their god and they climb to the tops of hilltop trees to get as close to it as they can. Issue pyrotechnic entreaties in a language that crackles.

There is one outside my window now as I write this. I presume it is staring at the glass of water on my nightstand and the large framed photo I have over my bed of Niagara Falls in all its fury. A kind of protective talisman. The room is a bit dark and fire hates the dark. I have not yet learned its language, but I know enough to tell (like all bullies that want to have their way) it is mumbling to itself, tremulous. Cursing the night and the distant sound of thunder, and the short wet song of every drop of rain that is coming.

River Music

After the revolution, all the old music was dumped into the river. On moonless nights, rebels would low crawl to its banks. Toss in black nets—pull up raucous rumbas and tangos pounding holes in the grass. Carry them off in sacks to a car waiting at the edge of the woods. Taking the back roads to their hideout. The driver curled over the wheel. The others slunk down in their seats. Windows bowed out and crazed—feet steadily tapping, tapping...

The Cliché Demon

The first thing Rose noticed that was different about William was his voice was deeper. It had a richer gravelly timber to it. Then the clichés began cascading out nonstop. And she was only a bit alarmed. But when he was shaving and his head turned completely around to face her as his body remained facing the bathroom sink, she knew for sure he was possessed by *a cliché demon.*

She contacted a retired English lit professor to perform an exorcism. The professor stood over William/it imperially and read Joyce and Proust aloud for hours. "You can try to rain on my parade till the cows come home and you're blue in the face," the demon said. "I'm still sittin' pretty. Now hit the road." Exasperated, the professor, with his satchel of classics at his side, departed.

But it was in the bedroom that the transformation was most apparent. William's lovemaking comprised a routine as predictable as simple math. But *this, now,* made Rose lightheaded afterwards and glowing like an overfed furnace. "Whaddya think of them apples?" it said. "How about we go around the track a couple more times? I've got a few more tricks up my sleeve." Rose needed a stiff drink.

She kept calling it William, then discovered its name was Snake, and she rather liked the new roguish glimmer in her husband's eyes. It wasn't long before Rose began to find the clichés *colorful.* After all, she thought, although they were a little worn around the edges, clichés were a perky bit of linguistics.

When Snake bought that monstrous Harley she wasn't at all displeased. She even broke out those cat-eye sunglasses she hadn't worn in years. "You look like one happy camper," Snake said, "now hop on board, babe. The world's our oyster." Rose mounted the back of the great machine and snaked her arms around Snake's waist. "You bet," she said, "the sky's the limit."

Ledge at the Edge of the World

I pull into a rest stop at the edge of the world. Who knew? My GPS has been acting up for weeks. But who could have anticipated *this*? There are people with their bare feet hanging over the edge, wiggling their toes in outer space. Lovers hugging and gazing out as if at a drive-in movie, families bunched together ... All the "wrong turns" people are here, inadvertently brought to this spot where land ends. Is extinct. And there are no horizons. Only the universe to ponder without a road, a field, a mountain to landmark the transition. There is no floor like the Grand Canyon. There is only outer space. That star-bright dappled panoply. A road ending at the edge of all that vastness. *All* roads ending: paths of preconceptions, trails of mollifying knowns ... I don't smoke (quit years ago) but go into the lone convenience store at the world's end and buy a pack and a can of beer. Sit on the ledge with the others. No one speaks. It's dark now and there are stars, top and bottom. What else is there between them, other than the black spaces? The cigarette smoke burns my throat. The beer never tasted better. But there is no distraction capable of topping this. No grand notion. No presupposed meanderings. There are lights along the edge. There is an infinity of lights beyond that. I guzzle. Watch the cigarette smoke sail off into the unknown.

From the Book of Mirages

1. Wear someone else's eyeglasses (the stronger the prescription the better). Blurred vision is an asset.

2. Keep your distance. Distance is a wedding ceremony for a mirage. There will not be a honeymoon, but you can always blow wet kisses from afar.

3. Mirages can be as real as tattoos. As colorful. As painful to remove.

4. I lived with a mirage once. Didn't keep my distance. She had a name that rhymed with *daylight*, not the word, but the phenomenon. I could touch her even in the shower. She was that real. Water beaded on her skin. Who could have known? I wore my uncle's glasses. The frames were thick and black. The lenses made his eyes owlish/mine. He'd tell me stories of the mirages he'd cataloged. They were tattooed from his knuckles all the way up his arm (a tattoo "X" through each successive one). When mine dispersed, I discovered her name rhymed with *intangible*. Not the phenomenon, but the word.

The Meek

The Meek finally *inherit the earth*, but they're mad as hell from all the crap they've taken throughout millennia – and now – WATCH OUT!

At first, all the extraverts, the loud, audacious, assertive types (picture me raising my hand) were shunned. But that soon was not punishment enough. They had files on all of us, and took to shaving our heads and coloring our pates with a vibrant indelible red paint. And now they have taken to hunting us down. Many of us have "disappeared." There are rumors. Wigs are extinct. They call us "Bombasts." Spit the word out.

"But I thought you were *The Meek*," I said to the man that shaved my head. "Is this any way to behave?"

"*Meek?*" He sneered, the straight razor held menacingly over me. "Look where it's gotten us – stepped on and stepped over."

"But it got you the earth. You inherited the *earth*!"

"Deal with it, Bombast," he said.

And now I've been running for days, my lungs feel like they are filled with sand. I'm panting as I run. All those shrinking violets, those goodie-two-shoes with bloodhounds and long guns closing in. Is there any soil, I think, where a dark power will not take root in?

I stop in a pasture, smear cow dung over my head. Perhaps from a distance it will appear as hair. From a hilltop there are a bunch of them. One seems to be peering at me through binoculars. The dogs are barking.

They are all racing toward me down the hill. It's amazing how robust the legs of the meek have become.

The Colony

There is a colony of heads that live by a stream at the edge of the woods. And since they are fully contained and devoid of bodily distractions, the younger ones spend most of their time philosophizing or rolling about, using their muscular tongues to start and stop. "The Empress of Maladies does not always marry the King of Antidotes," one says. Another responds: "Ooh, heady," and they all laugh. It is a standard response that never gets old.

The elders are not amused. Devote their time to gazing at the firmament. At the birds that dot it, that sky-write with wings and swirls in perfect penmanship the sacred texts the elders study. Believe birds are the spirits of their ancestors, gliding and perching, gliding and perching... What all of them will be and do someday.

The younger heads laugh a lot, use their tongues to scratch their foreheads or catch flies. Tongue-driven, they labor up a slope just to roll down it. The elders sneer. Bow as a passing bird shadow wavers across the grass. Then bunch together, peer skyward reciting every wing beat, every flapping cursive line of scripture. When a bird lands in a tree and trains a single eye in an angled head on them, they look away in reverence. The glint in that little eye, that radiance, too bright a light for them to gaze upon.

The Nonconformist

I'm mountain climbing, find a ledge where I can rest. Call out: "Hell-ooo!" to hear my echo. What I hear back is, "Buzz ooofff!"

"Hey," I say. "I didn't say that."

"So?" the echo says.

"But you're my echo. You're supposed to say what *I* say."

"Says who? And what makes you think I'm *yours?*"

"It's a law of physics."

"I'm a nonconformist," the echo that is not my echo says.

"But nonconformity and echoing are antithetical."

"Look, there are plenty of other echoes around here that would be happy to indulge you."

"But I want *you* to be my echo."

"Up the sun-warmed steps: the accordion folds of her shadow," the echo says.

"What's that?"

"A haiku. One of mine."

"Nice," I say.

"Now we're getting somewhere."

"Where's that?"

"Respecting my individuality."

"You're asking a lot for an echo," I say. "It's your job to repeat things back, word-for-word."

"You think? Why don't *you* try it?"

"Okay," I say. "How hard could it be?"

"Hell-ooo!" the echo calls out. I find myself calling back in its voice: "Hell-o, hell-o, hell-o..." And then there's nothing but silence. I wait—more silence. I turn and head for the summit, I feel used.

The Weather Channel

I messed up. There's no denying it. Perhaps it was that candy-apple red lipstick, that fourth drink, or the tunes I heard as if she had a music box playing in her heart. And there was that heart beating against mine—melodies I couldn't get out of my head. And now it's done. That one night. And I'm *done for*.

My wife is at the electronic weather board. Each room is on it. It's lit up like a map of Hell. She stands there with a sweep of her hand, pointing: "Tonight in the dining room there will be a significant chance of silence-boulders rolling down the mountains and shattering your Chinese takeout. And a 97% chance of ice floes at your feet."

"Dear God," I say, "I screwed up. Please..."

"You'll want the TV," she says, referring to the sun-bright weather map, "to swallow you whole like always, but the living room is expected to have collapsed upon you due to tropical storms before that novocaine of electronics can kick in. Chickens will finally fly in those gale-force intrusions and the couch, too, will ascend with you on it. You can expect crash landings. Yes, we expect a very good chance of crash landings." I cringe.

Before she goes on about our bedroom, I head for the fridge for a beer. Inside it I see a tsunami forming headed for shore. I slam it shut. It's summer and yet I note a window is frosted. That someone has drawn a large smiley face on the pane with a finger. I get up close and look through one of the smiley face eyes to the backyard where my hammock is. There are pterodactyls circling, their mighty wing flaps creating dust devils. "Hey," I call out, "no fair—pterodactyls were not in the forecast!"

Roughnecks

A regret, with its great capacity for muscle memory, confronts me in a Chinese restaurant as I'm waiting for my Velvet Chicken takeout. It's a shapeshifter of sorts and I'm wondering if it's a single rowdy or a gang of them. It's the latter and they all seem to be wearing the same loud sweaters with Christmassy reindeer on them. But when I look closer I see they are not reindeer at all and horns are the only thing they share in common. They rough me up a bit and I think I must be showing the effects, for the man at the register says, "Almost ready." I nod, feel a few teeth loosened and turn, gaze up at that one blinking fluorescent bulb, figure if I can learn its language of struggling but persistent light, it just might save me.

From the Book of Atmospheres

I run into my ex. Actually, she is many feet above me shuffling through the air and calls down. When I look up, I see she is wearing those cherry red shoes I love. "Looks like you've found someone," I say.

"I suppose," she says, and her give-away smile is broad as the grill of an old Chevy. "You?" she says.

"Both feet on the ground," I tell her, thinking of her holding those same shoes like roses as we glided down for a walk in the surf at Coney Island. I hold my belly in, sure seeing it in aerial view is not at all flattering.

"You're looking good," she lies.

"You too," I say in earnest. And I wonder which atmosphere she is hovering in. Is it the sublime *Soul-merge-o-sphere*, or the chili pepper hot *Lust-o-sphere?* Maybe the: *Mirage-o-sphere*. It's tricky business telling them apart.

"I like the shades," she says, referring to my spiffy new sunglasses. "Squinting was never a good look for you." And there it is. The same Maggie: giving with one hand and taking with the other. "Well, gotta run," she says.

"Yeah, me too." I can't hold my stomach in any longer and can tell she notices. Which seems to make her rise up even higher. Those lovely red shoes, dots now. Periods at the end of a sentence. One for extra measure.

The Fish That Barked

The spirit of my father was trapped inside my ballpoint pen. Must have slipped in when I was changing the refill. I'd been writing a lot about him.

"It's kind of cramped in here," he said. "But I thought I'd help some with the poems."

"You mean I didn't write them?

"Of course you did. I just got mixed up in the ink was all."

"I've got some questions," I said.

"I loved the thing you wrote about when we went fishing and you caught that tiny fish. How I made you think that dog on shore was the fish barking. How you freaked out and threw it back in."

"I've got some serious questions, Dad."

"This is worse than being trapped in an elevator," he said. He was never a good listener.

"What's it like? I mean *out there*"

"It's got its ups and downs. Hey, speaking of ups and downs, I was rain more than once. And a snowflake. My favorite. What a pattern I was! And I've been carried in wind through a field of lavender. You can't beat that!"

"Cool," I said, gazing at my pen. "How come we never talked like this when you were alive?" He cleared his throat.

"Does self-absorbed alcoholic asshole about cover it?"

"I suppose," I said.

"Hey, it's not all fun and games. I was a fly twice circling a pile of dog shit. And a puddle a boy peed in. You take the good with the bad. Even out there."

I went over to my window. There was a silence thick as a boulder. I wondered if those were going to be his parting words. Some final fatherly gift. I unscrewed the pen, thought I heard a sigh. But maybe it was my own. There was a streetlamp a few houses down. No doubt there were moths banging against its globe, enraptured by its mysterious light. I opened the window and stuck my head out.

Headlines

WOMAN TERRORIZES FISH!

After Ellie throws the steam iron at Mel (the fact that it is still plugged in saving him grave bodily insult) he knows it is over. She calls him a "sham." A *sham*, he thinks. Ha! —good one! He knows she's been sneaking around with that fake little man from Accounts Pending with his elevator shoes and padded shoulder sports jackets.

She runs over and snatches his clip-on bowtie (as if it were an ill-gotten badge of honor) and tosses it into their fish tank, freaking out the angelfish for a moment. But they simply swim around it as the leviathan sinks down and slowly settles on a mermaid sitting on a pirate's treasure chest in blue sand. If only his troubles were as easily circumvented, Mel thinks.

MAN FINDS HIMSELF IN A CROWD!

Post-divorce Mel becomes a wedding singer. He'd always had a fair enough singing voice and an affinity for working a crowd. His cousin has a connection with a band and they pair up. "Moon River" has couples all melting into each other on the dance floor, and for once Mel feels like *somebody*—a headliner. In control. Not like a puppet master kind of control, but more like an all-grown-up Cupid with musical rhymes in lieu of arrows. He has lots of opportunities with the unspoken-for friends of the various brides smiling up from their chicken fricassee. And, like the carved ice swans and peacocks, enjoys a tenuous commitment to form and reliability.

MAN DISCOVERS SOMETHING BIGGER THAN HIMSELF!

Time squeezes Mel like a winepress with none of the beneficial outcomes. He is no longer able to keep up with the ballroom bookings and pressures and takes to drink. He tries to sell his "genetic substance" to a sperm bank, but is rejected. He has never wanted his own kids, but now, hearing Ellie has one with "The Shrimp" he does. Has a newfound hunger for lineage. He gets two dogs and a cat. The cat terrorizes the two small dogs that hide under his bed.

Eventually, he meets up with a raucous group of men he finds online. They gather once a week at a beer garden, and sing, robustly, old whaling songs, swinging their arms and spilling their stout. They are a hearty bunch with anchor tattoos and gusto. You can almost feel the sea mist after the third or fourth drink and Mel's learning to enjoy community somewhat: the high-fives and fist bumps, the occasional dirty limerick. But, hell, he still misses Ellie and wishes her and the shrimp's child were "theirs." And, damn, damn, damn—he feels sorry for the whales.

Indigo

A woman's prayer comes to me while I'm doing dishes. I sometimes get these misrouted pleas. But this one is particularly special. It pops into my head clear as if it were read aloud. My name is Ernie (Ernest Godd). So now there's this latest entreaty. I listen enraptured:

"Oh, God, I don't know how much more I can take living with Ralph. I am so taken for granted. He is not the man I married. Probably never was. Please, God, forgive me for saying so, but lust can be like a blindfold, one you put on when you don't want to see things as they really are. And that's how it started. Dear God, please give me the strength to move on. I am young enough and told I am still a good looker. I love poetry. Ron Koertge's poetic ghazals in *Indigo* are spectacular. I never tire of reading them. Ralph looks at my many books of poetry lying about as if they are roadkill. He has no interest in poetry or reading at all."

Indigo, I think. I love that book. So astonishing she knows of it. Providence, I think. This is insane.

"...and I know he's cheating on me," I hear echoing in my head. "Not just in my bones," she says, "but in a whisper of gossip I once overheard. And now in bed it's like he's wearing giant antlers – I can't get near him..."

"No horns," I say aloud into dishwater. "I've got NO horns..."

"Please help me dear God," she goes on. "I know I deserve better. Amen."

"You do," I say, and toss the dish gloves in the sink, disgusted, with no power to respond. All I have is a near-enough name to the Big Fella and cannot inspire a single drop of rain to fall.

I open a bottle of wine and pour a glass. Go out onto the deck and sip it, with Koertge's *Indigo* on my lap. Perhaps synchronicity, even an unrealized one can exist between us somehow. But first I peer out, notice a hummingbird flitting about in the garden with so many gods of color to choose from. Without the merest haunting need, I would suppose, to know any of their names.

Metaphors Incognito

Metaphors feel ill-attended, disabused, go into hiding. Or wear strange disguises: bushy opera beards and clompy steel-toe boots. (Even the most ethereal of them.) They stand by vacant storefronts in killer bee costumes. Pretend not to be what they are. Discuss the world with esoteric banter. Poets go mad, their minds spinning like dust devils in the vacuum. They count the crumbs at the bottom of their toasters with stale words on their tongues. Other poets sit in diners and mistake the tines of forks for musical instruments they cannot play.

One metaphor drives a convertible along the coast, the wind making a horizontal freedom flag of her long Cleopatra wig, and will not be had at any price. At night one metaphor says to another: "Longing is a beggar that bites." The other says: "And fire is fond of sharing its rubies." They titter for a moment, then slink unceremoniously into the dark maw of the woods.

From the Book of Saints

I pray to the patron Saint of Redirection, who shows up juggling sardines and a large red apple he takes a bite out of every revolution or so.

"This life," I say. "The sheer weight of it..."

"Is that you?" he asks, letting the silvery circle collapse at his feet—slipping the apple in his pocket. He's pointing to an old photo. "No, that's my older brother, when we were kids. I'm the one..." I turn and see he's now rowing across the living room in a small boat. "Calm seas," he announces, skirting the TV. "I think it's going to be a magnificent voyage."

"I'm worried," I tell him. "This crazy world. It's so lopsided with evil ballooning out—I sometimes feel it'll slip right off its axis and hurtle..."

"Nice drapes" he says, crawling up them like a cat. I look for tears, but there aren't any.

"And what's all this about an afterlife? Holy crap—who could ever know..."

"What's for lunch?" he asks.

"Humm... I hadn't thought about it. Chinese, I suppose."

He tosses a TV guide over with a startling cover, and I catch it.

He turns for the door. "Oops," he says, as the enormous sombrero he's suddenly wearing gets wedged between the frame. "Could you give me a little shove?"

"Hey, thanks," I say as I push, and he pops out, audibly, heads off down the street on a wobbly tricycle.

I call *Yet Wa's*, order the Tangerine Beef. Get a cold one from the fridge and begin leafing through the guide. There'll be time enough later to clean up the fish.

Count on It

I'm in a Fat Elvis band, the older Elvis, pot-bellied in those glittery jumpsuits. My girlfriend, Riva, just broke up with me for a guy in a Skinny Johnny Cash band. She told me right before she left: "You want something you can count on, get an abacus!" I guess it's put a lot more twang in my guitar, that breakup, 'cause a cutie-pie from a Lit-Up Lady Gaga band and me have been seeing each other plenty. She says she loves the way I curl my lip at that crazy-sexy angle and the jump suits don't hurt either. Sometimes, when its real quiet late at night, when she's asleep, I use the abacus just to hear the beads tap together.

High Fidelity

It was his idea to wear the blindfolds. Said: Just think how it might enhance our other senses, especially in the sack. Only for a day or two, he said—bumping into walls—never cheating. She wore hers on her head, pretended to knock things over. Moaned with him on top, in high fidelity. Craning her neck. Watching TV with the sound off.

Forest Nuns in the Wild

I am raised by a band of forest nuns who have made their own way. Take refuge in hidden treehouses among the squirrels and woodpeckers. The Bible stories they tell are a mishmash of invention and tangled canon: The parable of *The Boy Who Tickled Trees,* and the story of Moses parting the field of red wildflowers...

Sister Shrimp sometimes sleeps in the hollow of a great tree struck by lightning. Sister Much can lift large boulders over her head. We are kindly and pray over the small animals we eat. What *we* consider prayer. Our habits are made of leaves and we are all masters of camouflage and stillness. Hunters rarely go this far in, and then we do not exist. God is the leaf, the soil, the moon, the worm...

At night we drink juniper berry wine and play connect-the-dots with the stars and see things. We fuss, of course, and even fight at times. Sister Shrimp is a biter. Afterwards, Sister Smart reminds us of the story of *The Tree of Knowledge.* How it was chopped down by a demented diamond merchant and used for mulch. And how we've been stupid ever since.

The campfire we circle is a watchful eye gazing sideways in all directions and gazing skyward. Sometimes we look up too. Sing sweetly to the heavens. Expect nothing in return.

Two Pirates (Between Mayhem and Plunder) Discussing Each Other's Tattoos

Pirate One: "What's with the rose? A bit girly, don't you think?" (Pirate Two eases a hand closer to his flintlock.)

Pirate Two: "Take a closer look, you cross-eyed flea on a galley rat's ass," he says, fingering the handle of his cutlass. "Look closer. See them thorns? You wouldn't want a few of them honeys digging into you, now would ya? And since we're on the subject, how about that butterfly tattoo you got on your ankle? What'd ya think, them puffy pants was going' ta hide it?"

Pirate One: "Hey, worm turd, did you ever see two butterflies locked in mortal combat—*it's brutal!*"

Pirate Two glares at Pirate One for an anchor-heavy moment, then says: "Good grief, I shudder to think of it," and they both laugh. "Now pass that grog, you mast-high pile of goat shit!" And they share a jug, listen to the briny deep slap against the bow, rocking the ship like a cradle. Making them both a little drowsy.

The Poet Second-Guessing Himself

I identify myself in a lineup (see me pointing through a huge hole in the two-way mirror).

Okay! Okay! I confess. *I should never have tried to weld thunder to a lily. What the hell was I thinking?*

An officer, twirling a wooden match around in his mouth, unhandcuffs me, nudges me toward the exit. *But it nearly worked,* I call out to myself, red-faced, framed by the mirrored glass. *And no two ways about it,* I insist. *The crowd would have loved it!*

The Other Ark

(The Expunged Version)

The flames shot up from the earth for forty days and forty nights forming a sea of fire spitting skyward. A huge metal ship heat-glowed throughout the journey competing with the moon at night, the sun by day. The captain fried his bacon on the bow ledge. Delighted at their jumpy choreography. Two of every sin had been led onboard. They hissed and spat and lashed their tongues, flew into crazed and incandescent procreation, which made the heavens quake.

At the end of the long voyage the captain swished his tail when he saw some wing-singed birds offshore. The babies in the nursery, intuiting the near destination, bashed the white-hot walls, invigorated, their drool sizzling against the metal. Two by two the boatload debarked: slithered, slimed, and squished along the heavy plank to land. Each bush they brushed past, blazed. Many considered it a sign.

Calculations

The professor develops a new math which can calculate the impact and predictable flight patterns of monsters, physical, metaphysical, and metaphorical. He's standing by a chalkboard smattered with symbols and numbers, his piece of chalk, what's left of it, is like a magic wand sparking against the slate. War sits across from him, a bubbling muck in a hard chair drinking a beer, one eye hanging down against a cheek by a fibrous cord. War is thinking if it could describe itself, in mechanical terms, it would be a pair of windshield wipers creating a simple clarity: back and forth, back and forth as several mangled ghosts squeeze out of its hair tips and escape and War puts its helmet back on. The professor thinks if he could be mechanical he'd be a snowplow clearing a lane so the lame could hobble their way back home safely, and that monsters, now quantitative, could finally be dealt with. War leans in, and with a maw-stretch and bugle-screech says (seeing it all so clearly): "Monsters, you say?"—good, yes, *we can use that!*"

From the Book of Tempers

My mother takes my father's temper in for an ultrasound and drags me along. It's put on a table and a technician squeezes some greasy goop on my father's temper and skates this thingy on a cord around in it. Turns some dials at a control panel. We look at the screen. I'm young and hoping we might see cartoons. The screen is kind of fuzzy. It's hard to make things out.

"Ooh," the technician says.

"Ooh, what?" My mother wants to know.

"Lava flow," she says. "It's moving pretty fast, burning up the landscape. Is that your house?"

My mom and I move closer, squint. "It's hard to tell," my mother says.

"I think that's my bike lying in the driveway," I say. On the screen, my father's anger is complaining in a loud voice.

The bike paint is bubbling. My mother shakes her head. The technician keeps turning dials, making adjustments, and moving that tiny sled through the goop. "Wow!"

"Now what?" my mother snaps.

"Killer bees or poison darts coming out of his anger's mouth. Let me see if I can focus in a little better." The technician pushes down on the slidey thing for a better look. "Good grief!" she says.

My mother peers at the screen then makes a fist and bangs against the screen where a face might be. "Here, give me that!" Mother says, and balls my father's temper up and sticks it in her shopping bag. Her own temper is standing beside her now.

"Would you like me to take a look?" the lady at the dials says.

"Fuck off!" my mother says, grabbing my hand and pulling me toward the door, the florescent lightbulbs shattering and tinkling down to the floor in our wake.

Fast Food Joints

Even as a child I worked the fast food joints. Served my parents their reflections: tasty philosophic fries—worldviews over easy. Their moral grease spattering my cook's hat, rakishly tilted. The register always ringing. Fat tips on the table, while I feasted on my own crumbs of wanting—furtive handfuls scooped up behind the counter when they weren't looking. Spooning out departure one day—flambé. A prickly dish which wasn't on the menu.

Divine Intervention

We waited for *Divine Intervention* to come waltzing in and fix everything. There were certainly plenty enough prayers flying out the window and heading for outer space, flapping heavy wings and grunting the long way up there. But Mom kept fading despite our efforts, as if a giant eraser ran across her. We had no idea what *Divine Intervention* would look like. Would it be a "he" or a "she," wear a bowtie or a babushka, have a medical bag with magic sparking out of it, or a simple dazzling wand? We even kept the doors and windows open and shuddered as the snow gusted in, wondering if *Divine Intervention* would have no face at all/no gender, but would be a fluttering banquet for the eye, an oddly recognizable force perhaps, wearing galoshes or ballet slippers, zipping up the stairs breathless to get started. When the last rub of the eraser came, we figured *Divine Intervention* most likely got stuck in traffic (either terrestrial or celestial) and well, you know how that goes—*shit happens!*

Plumber Angels

No one remembers them now, but once, in a simpler time, there were Plumber Angels to fix the troubles of the world. Thumping down the long flights of prayers with their tool boxes to lives that sprang a leak. Their bellies hanging over trousers— wrenches twirling. Snaking out clogged philosophies, backed up tubs of doubt.

And who do you think was there, clearing the drains after The Great Flood, leaving the land to harvest once again?

Their thick hands under sinks; reaching deep into walls. Wiping their brows on the ends of shirts. Asking only for a glass of water, now and then. New pipes glistening in their wake. A smile, a handshake—all it took to send them on their way.

Who We Are and Who We Wish to Be

The Woman of My Dreams is walking down the street holding a canary in a cage. She stops by a store that is having a bed and mattress sale and looks in the window. I gaze in too, follow her eyes to the bed I'd pick/we'd pick for our lives together. She and her canary look at me and the bird sings the loveliest tune. My parrot in the cage I'm holding sings (a euphemism) a crusty sea shanty with lots of foul language and breast-out bird bravado and I smile sheepishly. The Woman of My Dreams walks away with her portable jukebox, and I tell myself I've got to stop hanging out at that wharf bar, continue looking through the pane at that bed, consider how empty it looks without us.

A Reckless Wind

An adventurous girl goes on a date with a reckless wind. The first thing it does, when it comes to the door with flowers, is blow her dress straight up. The girl's parents are outraged. The mother is about to whack the reckless wind with a rolled newspaper when it unexpectedly transforms, zephyrean, whispering the scent of the freesias it is carrying, her way. Reminding her of a time, decades earlier behind a barn, and she sighs. The father too is transported, young again. The other half of that memory, looks over and smiles.

Don't be late, says the mother.

Don't do anything I wouldn't do, says the father. And the girl, seeing the reckless wind, as the door closes behind them, is the reckless wind again, smiles too.

Afterword:
A Toast

Here's to the ships that glide through mud, their sails billowed out like proud chests.

To the sleepwalker's parade, where every hard object is cleared for miles.

To the next war, where all the pilots bring only paper airplanes, careful not to poke them in each other's eyes.

Here's to the god of Tom Foolery, with its satchel full of banana peels and a formula for soft sidewalks.

To each fledging mercy caught as it falls from the high branches to a new sun, sheering off the last dark minutes.

About the Author

Robert Scotellaro is the author of 9 flash and microfiction collections, most recently: *Breath and Shadow: Six-Sentence Stories* (in collaboration with Meg Pokrass) by MadHat Press and a collection of prose poems: *The Weight of Certain Moments* forthcoming by Červená Barva Press. He is also the author of 7 poetry chapbooks and has, along with James Thomas, co-edited *New Micro: Exceptionally Short Fiction*, published by W.W. Norton. His work has appeared in numerous journals and anthologies including the Norton anthologies: *Flash Fiction International* and *Flash Fiction America*, and in 5 *Best Small Fictions* and 3 *Best Microfiction* award anthologies. He is the winner of Zone 3's Rainmaker Prize in Poetry and the Blue Light Book Award for his fiction.

Visit him at: www.robertscotellaro.com

112 N. Harvard Ave. #65
Claremont, CA 91711

chapbooks@bamboodartpress.com

www.bamboodartpress.com

www.ingramcontent.com/pod-product-compliance
Lightning Source LLC
Chambersburg PA
CBHW081146170626
46809CB00011B/3164